PARK COUNTY PUBLIC LIBRARY
GUFFEY BRANCH

Celebration Food

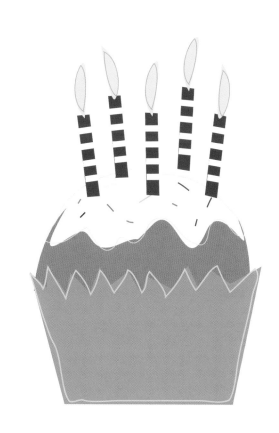

Clare Hibbert

PARK COUNTY PUBLIC LIBRARY
GUFFEY BRANCH

Cherrytree books are distributed in the United States
by Black Rabbit BooksP.O. Box 3263, Mankato, MN, 56002

U.S. publication copyright © Cherrytree Books 2008
International copyright reserved in all countries. No part of
this book may be reproduced in any form without written
permission from the publisher.
Printed in China by WKT Company Ltd.

Library of Congress Cataloging-in-Publication Data
Hibbert, Clare, 1970-
  Celebration food / Clare Hibbert. -- 1st ed.
      p. cm. -- (Sparklers)
  Originally published: London : Evans Brothers Ltd., 2007.
  Includes index.
  Summary: "Covers a range of celebrations from around the
world, both religious and secular, and the foods eaten on those occasions.
Includes simple recipe"--Provided by publisher.
  ISBN-13: 978-1-84234-530-6
  ISBN-10: 1-84234-530-3
  1. Holiday cookery--Juvenile literature. 2. Cookery, International--Juvenile literature. 3.
Fasts and feasts--Juvenile literature. I. Title. II. Series.

TX739.H53 2009
641.5'68--dc22

                                                        2007046384

First edition
9 8 7 6 5 4 3 2 1

First published in 2007 by Evans Brothers Ltd.
2A Portman Mansions, Chiltern Street, London W1U 6NR, United Kingdom

Produced for Evans Brothers Limited by
White-Thomson Publishing Ltd.

Copyright © Evans Brothers Limited 2007
Educational consultant: Sue Palmer MEd FRSA FEA
Project manager: Clare Hibbert
Picture research: Amy Sparks
Design: Balley Design Limited
Creative director: Simon Balley
Designer/Illustrator: Michelle Tilly

Contents

Special Days

Celebrations are special days...

Spring Festivals

hop

Where would you look

for Easter eggs?

6

eggs

candies

apples

These goodies are for an Iranian spring festival.

7

Weddings

bride

groom

This couple cuts a cake at their wedding...

8

...and **this** couple shares a **drink**.

9

Harvest Festival

What would **you** take to a harvest festival?

10

Thanksgiving dinner is a special harvest celebration.

Christmastime

How would you decorate Christmas cookies?

Yummy!

PARK COUNTY PUBLIC LIBRARY
CODY BRANCH

This **Christmas bread** looks a bit like a **crown**!

13

Id ul-Fitr

mosque

Muslims share a feast for Id...

dates

cheese-filled cakes

...and eat sweet treats.

Divali

Divali is the **festival** of lights.

16

Indian candies

Hindus offer food in the temple.

People eat roast duck

at Chinese New Year...

18

...and give lucky

tangerines as presents.

19

Make It: Charoset

Mix these things together to make charoset.

- grated apples ✓
- dates and raisins ✓
- apple juice ✓
- cinnamon ✓

Mmmmm!

This **treat** is **eaten** for

Jewish **Pesach.**

21

Notes for Adults

Sparklers books are designed to support and extend the learning of young children. The books' high-interest subjects broaden young readers' knowledge and interests, making them idea teaching tools as well.

Themed titles
Celebration Food is one of four ***Food We Eat*** titles that explore food and meals from around the world. The other titles are:
Let's Eat Breakfast   Let's Eat Lunch   Let's Eat Dinner

Areas of learning
Each ***Food We Eat*** title introduces educational concepts (such as personal development, literacy and mathematical skills) with subtlety and care. Children increase their knowledge and understanding of the world while developing their creativity.

Reading together
When sharing this book with younger children, take time to explore the pictures together. Encourage children by asking them to find, identify, count or describe different objects. Point out different colors or textures.

Allow quiet spaces in your reading so that children can ask questions or repeat your words. Try pausing mid-sentence so children can predict the next word. This sort of participation develops early reading skills.

Follow the words with your finger as you read them aloud. The main text is in Infant Sassoon, a clear, friendly font specially designed for children learning to read and write. The labels and sound effects on the pages add fun, engage the reader, and give children the opportunity to distinguish between different levels of communication. Where appropriate, labels, sound effects, or main text may be presented in phonic spelling. Encourage children to imitate the sounds.

As you read the book, you can also take the opportunity to talk about the book itself with appropriate vocabulary, such as "page," "cover," "back," "front," "photograph," "label," and "page number."

You can also extend children's learning by using the books as a springboard for discussion and further activities. There are a few suggestions on the facing page.

22

Pages 4–5: Special Days
Give each child an outline drawing of a cupcake to decorate and cut out. Write on the name and birthday of the child. Position on a birthday calendar mural, with the cakes sorted into the right months.

Pages 6–7: Spring Festivals
Mix crushed shredded wheat and melted chocolate and allow the children to shape the (cooled) mixture into nests to hold chicks or small chocolate eggs. Develop the theme of animal homes, for example through the song "Over in the meadow."

Pages 8–9: Weddings
Make a model bride and groom. Use clothes pins for bodies, wool for hair, and fabric and tissue paper for clothes and flowers.

Pages 10–11: Harvest Festival
Fill a basket with real fruits and vegetables for a harvest display. Taking turns, children can be blindfolded, take something from the basket, and then try to identify it by touch and smell.

Pages 12–13: Christmastime
Find out what children's favorite Christmas foods are, and compile a pictorial recipe book. Decorate its cover with a collage of Christmassy angels, bells, stars, and holly leaves.

Pages 14–15: Id ul-Fitr
Id ul-Fitr marks the end of Ramadan, the Muslim month of fasting. Make hilal (crescent moon and star) decorations. Use gold foil for each star and silver foil for each moon. Use string to link them and for hanging.

Pages 16–17: Divali
At Divali, Hindus and Sikhs light up their homes and sometimes set off fireworks. Make firework pictures. Scribble all over paper in different colored crayons, then cover with black crayon. Use fingernails or a coin to scratch away bits of black to create a colorful fireworks display.

Pages 18–19: Chinese New Year
In Chinese folk religion, each year is associated with an animal. Make cards for a pairs game, using pictures of the 12 animals: pig, rat, ox, tiger, rabbit, dragon, snake, horse, sheep, monkey, rooster, and dog.

Pages 20–21: Make It: Charoset
Pesach celebrates the escape of the Jews from slavery in Egypt. Jews eat charoset to remember the building mortar used by slaves. Use cuboid and triangular blocks to build Egyptian-style flat-roofed homes and pyramids.

IndeX

PARK COUNTY PUBLIC LIBRARY
GUFFEY BRANCH

Picture acknowledgments:
Alamy: 7 (Richard Levine), 9 (Photo Network), 10 (archivberlin/Fotoagentur/GmbH), 17 (ArkReligion.com); **Corbis:** 4–5 (Fabio Cardoso), 6 (© Ariel Skelley/Blend Images), 11 (Larry Williams), 12 (Ralf Hirschberger/dpa), 14 (Kazuyoshi Nomachi), 16 (Ken Seet), 19 (Franklin Lau); **Getty**: 8 (Ryan McVay/Stone); **iStockphoto:** cover balloons (Vasiliki Varvaki), cover tablecloth, 2–3, 13, 22–24 (Jon Helgason), cover, 13 (Andres Balcazar), cover sky, 22–24 (Judy Foldetta), 15 (Paul Cowan), 15 tablecloth (Gaffera); **Photolibrary:** 18 (Peter Brooks), 20–21 (Foodpix).